TEAM SPIRIT

'Alexander! What's *wrong* with you?' cried Lenny, shaking him. 'You're costing us the match!'

Alexander just stood there, staring at Lenny. His eyes had gone a dark black colour and the horrible smell was getting worse.

'Alexander! I'm asking you a question!' Lenny repeated, shaking him again.

James just stared quietly at the goalkeeper. He put his hand on Lenny's shoulder and led him away.

'We won't be a minute, Alexander!' he called back. 'Just going to talk tactics!'

James had to force Lenny along. His friend made no effort to walk on his own. He was quivering, mouth open, pointing at Alexander.

'A-A-Alexander!' he gasped under his breath. 'He's a g-g-ghost!'

St Sebastian's School in Grimesford is the pits. No, really — it is.

Every year, the high school sinks a bit further into the boggy plague pit beneath it and, every year, the ghosts of the plague victims buried underneath it become a bit more cranky.

Egged on by their spooky ringleader, Edith Codd, they decide to get their own back — and they're willing to play dirty. *Really* dirty.

They kick up a stink by causing as much mischief as inhumanly possible so as to get St Sebastian's closed down once and for all.

But what they haven't reckoned on is year-seven new boy, James Simpson and his friends Alexander and Lenny.

The question is, are the gang up to the challenge of laying St Sebastian's paranormal problem to rest, or will their school remain forever frightful?

There's only one way to find out . . .

TOO GHOUL FOR SCHOOL

TEAM SPIRIT

B. STRANGE

DEAN

DEAN

First published in Great Britain 2007 by Farshore
This edition published in Great Britain 2021 by Dean

An imprint of HarperCollins*Publishers*
1 London Bridge Street, London SE1 9GF
www.farshore.co.uk

HarperCollins*Publishers*
1st Floor, Watermarque Building, Ringsend Road
Dublin 4, Ireland

Text and Illustrations © 2007 Farshore
Text by Tommy Donbavand
Illustrations by Pulsar Studio (Beehive Illustration)

ISBN 978 0 6035 8093 2
Typeset by Avon DataSet Ltd, Bidford on Avon, Warwickshire
Printed and bound in Great Britain by the CPI Group
001

A CIP catalogue record for this title is available from the British Library.

MIX
Paper from
responsible sources
FSC C007454

This book is produced from independently certified FSC™ paper
to ensure responsible forest management.
For more information visit: www.harpercollins.co.uk/green

Special thanks to:
Matt Crossick, St John's Walworth Church of England Primary School and Belmont Primary School

School versus . . .

Year-seven new boy
and chief spook-hunter

James Simpson

Headmaster's son
and official brainiac

Alexander Tick

Strong as an ox,
gentle as an
unusually tall lamb

Lenny Maxwell

...Ghoul!

Loud-mouthed ringleader of the plague-pit ghosts

Edith Codd

Young ghost and a secret wannabe St Sebastian's pupil

William Scroggins

Bone idle ex-leech merchant with a taste for all things gross

Ambrose Harbottle

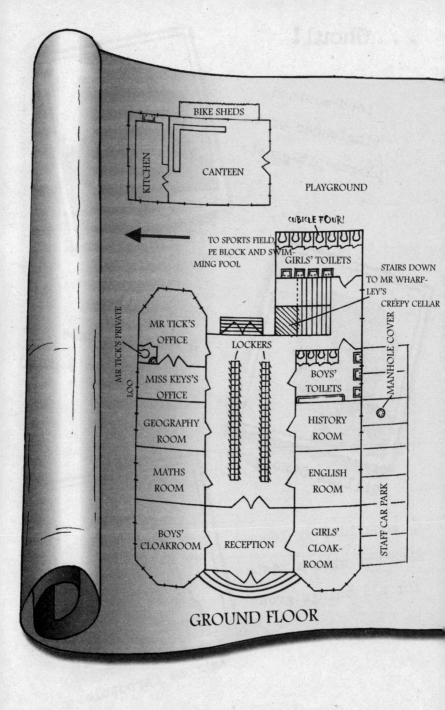

BIKE SHEDS

KITCHEN

CANTEEN

PLAYGROUND

CUBICLE FOUR!

TO SPORTS FIELD, PE BLOCK AND SWIMMING POOL

GIRLS' TOILETS

STAIRS DOWN TO MR WHARPLEY'S CREEPY CELLAR

MR TICK'S PRIVATE LOO

MR TICK'S OFFICE

LOCKERS

MANHOLE COVER

MISS KEYS'S OFFICE

BOYS' TOILETS

GEOGRAPHY ROOM

HISTORY ROOM

MATHS ROOM

ENGLISH ROOM

STAFF CAR PARK

BOYS' CLOAKROOM

RECEPTION

GIRLS' CLOAK-ROOM

GROUND FLOOR

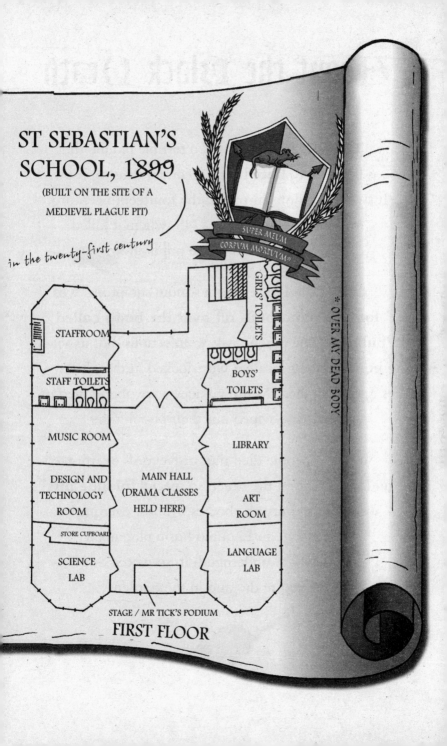

ST SEBASTIAN'S
SCHOOL, 1~~1899~~

(BUILT ON THE SITE OF A
MEDIEVEL PLAGUE PIT)

in the twenty-first century

SUPER MEUM
CORPUM MORTUUM*

* OVER MY DEAD BODY

STAFFROOM

STAFF TOILETS

MUSIC ROOM

DESIGN AND
TECHNOLOGY
ROOM

STORE CUPBOARD

SCIENCE
LAB

MAIN HALL
(DRAMA CLASSES
HELD HERE)

GIRLS' TOILETS

BOYS'
TOILETS

LIBRARY

ART
ROOM

LANGUAGE
LAB

STAGE / MR TICK'S PODIUM

FIRST FLOOR

About the Black Death

The Black Death was a terrible plague that is believed to have been spread by fleas on rats. It swept through Europe in the fourteenth century, arriving in England in 1348, where it killed over one third of the population.

One of the Black Death's main symptoms was **foul-smelling boils all over the body called 'buboes'**. The plague was so infectious that its victims and their families were locked in their houses until they died. Many villages were abandoned as the disease wiped out their populations.

So many people died that graveyards overflowed and bodies lay in the street, so special **'plague pits'** were dug to bury the bodies. Almost every town and village in England has a plague pit somewhere underneath it, so watch out when you're digging in the garden . . .

Dear Reader

As you may have already guessed, B. Strange is not a real name.

The author of this series is an ex-teacher who is currently employed by a little-known body called the Organisation For Spook Termination (Excluding Demons), or O.F.S.T.(E.D.). 'B. Strange' is the pen name chosen to protect his identity.

Together, we felt it was our duty to publish these books, in an attempt to save innocent lives. The stories are based on the author's experiences as an O.F.S.T.(E.D.) inspector in various schools over the past two decades.

Please read them carefully - you may regret it if you don't . . .

Yours sincerely
The Publisher.

PS - Should you wish to file a report on any suspicious supernatural occurrences at your school, write to us and we'll pass it on to O.F.S.T.(E.D.) for you.

PPS - All characters' names have been changed to protect the identity of the individuals. Any similarity to actual persons, living or undead, is purely coincidental.

CONTENTS

CHAPTER 1
SAFE HANDS

'OOOOF!'

Alexander Tick winced as the football crunched into his stomach.

'Rubbish! You could have caught that one!' yelled his friend, James Simpson, from across the street. 'Sorry, did that hurt, mate?'

Alexander was writhing around on the ground, gasping for breath.

'No, you idiot!' he wheezed, pulling himself to his feet. 'I was practising my break-dancing. Of *course* it hurt!'

James shrugged. 'Well, maybe you should try

actually *catching* the ball this time?' he suggested,
taking another shot at Alexander.

'OOOOOOARGH!'

Alexander lunged at the ball, but it slapped him
hard in the face and he went flying across the
pavement. James sighed, and watched silently as
his friend climbed out of a prickly-looking hedge.

'I nearly got that one, didn't I?' Alexander

whimpered, pulling a leaf out of his hair.

'No, Stick,' sighed James. 'You nearly destroyed that garden. Now come here and let me give you a secret goalkeeping tip.'

Alexander crossed the street, rearranging his blazer. 'A secret tip? Where'd you hear it?' he asked.

'From a professional goalie I met,' James said, putting his arm round the friend's shoulders. 'You sure you're ready for it?'

Alexander nodded. 'I need all the advice I can get – the year-seven cup final's only two days off!'

James leant in close to Alexander and lowered his voice. 'Right. Here's the secret. It'll really help.'

Alexander nodded again.

'It's a sure-fire way to improve your skills,' James whispered, deadly serious.

Alexander nodded and held his breath.

'KEEP YOUR EYES *OPEN*, YOU IDIOT!' James bellowed at the top of his voice in Alexander's ear.

'AAAAAAAAAAAAARGH!' Alexander cried, almost jumping out of his skin.

James doubled over laughing, clutching his sides. He was still giggling when the third member of their gang, Lenny Maxwell, rounded the corner of the street.

'What's going on, you two?' Lenny said, lumbering up to them with his hands in his pockets. 'Why've you got leaves in your hair, Alexander?'

James wiped the tears from his eyes and slapped Lenny on the back.

'Just giving Alexander some training for the cup final!' he snorted, struggling to get his laughter under control. 'But he's still scared of the ball! Maybe you can talk some sense into him Lenny . . .'

Lenny raised his eyebrows and looked down at Alexander.

'You know, Stick, the ball's the least of your worries. It's our opponents you should be panicking about. St Mary's are a real bunch of leg-breakers!' Lenny said, reassuringly.

James stared at Lenny in mock surprise. 'Good one, Lenny!' he said, sarcastically. 'That'll really build up his confidence!'

'Well, it's true!' cried Lenny. 'They're terrifying! The smallest member of their team is bigger than me, and they got banned from the cup last year for sticking a corner flag up the referee's . . . OWWWW! What was *that* for?'

James had given Lenny a sharp kick to the shin.

'To shut you up!' said James, nodding at Alexander, who was shaking like a leaf. 'Look at him!'

'Well, St Mary's must be pretty tough!' Lenny said to James as they walked. 'We're only in the cup final cos no other school would play them!'

Alexander moped along a few paces behind the other two.

'Why, oh, *why* do I have to play in goal?' he wailed. 'I'm virtually allergic to any sort of sport!

Last summer I had to have a week off school after a particularly energetic game of chess, remember?'

James ruffled Alexander's hair.

'You know why you're in the team, Stick!' he said. 'Cos Ben "Safe Hands" Fletcher broke his finger last week, and you're our reserve!'

Lenny shuddered. 'Yeah, that was nasty. Picking his nose when the school bus crashed . . . Imagine the pain!' he muttered, rubbing his own nose for comfort.

Alexander scowled at them both. 'I'm only substitute goalie cos my dad's the headmaster!' he complained. 'He *made* me sign up! I never thought I'd actually have to *play*! I *hate* football!'

James began juggling the ball on his knee as he walked along. 'You hate all sorts of stuff, Stick,' he said, flicking the ball over a passing paper boy. 'Music, sport, games, weekends, holidays, fun . . .'

'Oh, shut up!' grumbled Alexander. 'I just enjoy the more intellectual things in life, that's all – like chemistry, biology and physics. I'll have you know, I had a great weekend studying the effects of sodium on . . . OOOF!'

The ball hit Alexander right in the chest, taking his breath away and making him drop his schoolbag.

'How about studying the effects of a football on the human body, Stick?' James laughed.

'I'll study the effects of my foot on your backside in a minute!' gasped Alexander, giving James a dead arm.

'Aaaaargh!' James wailed. 'How does someone as weedy as you give such bad dead arms, Stick?'

Alexander smirked to himself. 'Cos I studied the muscles of the upper arm in my biology textbook last night!' he smiled.

'Knock it off, you two!' Lenny shouted. 'This is important! We've got to play a team that beat us thirty-seven–nil last year in just two days' time. Could we please focus on our football practice?'

James just dribbled round Lenny and ran off down the street. 'Practice? I don't need practice!'

he yelled over his shoulder. 'I'm the super-striker that's gonna save the day! Hat-trick here I come!'

Lenny and Alexander watched him disappear off up the street. Lenny looked down at his shorter friend.

'Come on!' he said, trying to cheer him up. 'How about telling me one of your famous jokes?'

Alexander smiled. He loved jokes almost as much as he hated sport.

'Well, if you will twist my arm . . . Why do babies make great footballers?' he grinned.

Lenny shrugged his shoulders.

'Cos they're always dribbling!' Alexander cried.

Lenny rolled his eyes.

'I don't care how nasty St Mary's are, Stick,' he complained as they reached the school gates, 'playing them can't be any worse than listening to your gags!'

Mr Tick stood at the school gates with his hands on his hips.

'Come along!' he bellowed down the street at the hordes of reluctant pupils trudging into school.

He watched as his son and two other boys larked about all the way down the grimy old street that led to St Sebastian's.

'Alexander! That means you, too!' he shouted.

Mr Tick was not in a good mood. He liked to get at least three games of solitaire in before the school day started, but the school secretary, Miss Keys, had interrupted him twice that morning and he hadn't finished a single one.

He frowned as he saw James run through the gates with his school jumper over his head. *Why can't Alexander be a bit more sporty?* he thought to himself. *Oh, well. I'm sure a spell in the school football team will toughen him up!*

'Hurry up, you boys,' he roared, 'or you'll be in detention all week!'

Mr Tick checked his tie in a car mirror,

smoothed his hair down and inspected his teeth.

'Looking smart, headmaster,' he told his reflection. 'Very sharp indeed!'

He was so busy preening himself that he didn't notice a thick blob of stinking, gooey slime appear from thin air and land with a dollop on one of his Italian leather shoes.

He didn't even notice as it oozed round his shoe, giving off a foul, deadly stench. He was far too busy striding importantly back to his office. If he hurried, he might get a game of solitaire in before assembly started.

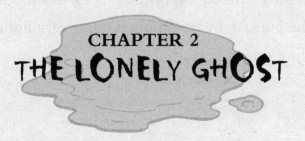

CHAPTER 2
THE LONELY GHOST

William Scroggins perched on top of the school gates, sulkily flicking bits of green slime off his decomposing arm. He was fed up. You'd think that after 600 years William would have got used to being a ghost, but he still hated it. The worst bit was having to stay invisible whenever he came above ground, in case the sight of his skeletal, rotting body terrified the children he wished could be his friends.

'Yuck!' he muttered, flicking some more slime off his arm. That was the second worst part of being a ghost, he decided. The sewer under St Sebastian's School that William, along with the other plague

victims buried in the pit underneath it, called home was filled with some pretty unpleasant stuff.

'Ooops!'

A particularly big dollop of slime flew off William's finger and landed right on the headmaster's shoe. William held his breath.

'Don't notice! Don't notice!' he mumbled to himself, tensely. Luckily for the young ghost, Mr Tick strode away without looking down.

'Phew!' William sighed, jumping off the gates. 'That was a close one!'

It wasn't just the pupils and the headmaster he had to hide from, either. If the rotten leader of the plague-pit ghosts, Edith Codd, had discovered William was hanging around the school again she'd make his life (or rather death) a misery. But William just couldn't help it. He hated it down in the gruesome sewer, and longed to be a pupil at St Sebastian's – with *real* friends, a *real* uniform and a *real*, solid body.

There were three boys at the school he particularly wanted to hang out with. A small, pale boy called Alexander (who looked not unlike William had done before the plague carried him off) and his two friends: a tall, friendly boy called Lenny, and the confident gang leader, James.

William spent a lot of his time drifting around

the school behind these three mates, pretending he was one of them. Of course, they never saw him. But he liked to pretend all the same.

'Here they come!' William said to himself, as he spotted Alexander and Lenny stroll through the school gates. James had already run ahead of them with a football. The two bigger boys seemed to be laughing at Alexander about something. William double-checked he was still invisible, and drifted up next to them. If only he could join in the fun!

Lenny was doing an impression of Alexander, waving his arms about his head and dropping a football. Alexander didn't look too pleased, but William found it hilarious. In fact, he laughed so hard that he forgot to keep up his invisibility for a split second.

'EEEEEEEEEEEEEEEEK!'

Thud.

A year-eight girl walking the other way must have caught a glimpse of him and fainted. William pulled himself together. That was the second close call of the day and school hadn't even started yet!

He concentrated hard and set off after the three boys again. James was talking.

'Oh, don't worry, Stick!' he said, as the boys walked down the corridor to their classroom. 'We'll do some more footy practice after school, and you'll be fine in the cup final!'

William leant in closer. They were talking about football – his favourite game in the world, ever! Back when he was alive, William had spent every Sunday playing football on the field outside his village. He had loved grabbing the thick, pig's bladder ball, fighting off the other team and punching it into the opposition's goal.

'Yeah!' Lenny chipped in. 'You'll make a great goalie! Just wait and see!'

A goalie? What's a goalie? thought William. He wondered if football had changed a bit since his day. Back then, anyone could use their hands, and the matches were more like big fights than sporting events.

In fact, he was so deep in thought that he drifted clean into a wall of school lockers. As he strug-
gled to drift back again, an unfortunate year-nine
girl opened her locker door to find William's grimy
hand dripping slime over her textbooks.

'EEEEEEEEEEEEK!'

THUD.

William concentrated hard on his invisibility
and drifted over her limp body. He really had to
be more careful.

James, Lenny and Alexander were about to en-
ter their classroom as he caught them up again.

'After all,' James was saying to Alexander,
'we've got a whole two days till the cup final.'

William could hardly contain his excitement.
That must be some kind of super-important football match! It sounded like fun!

'EEEEEEEEEEEEEEEEEEEEEEEEEK!'

THUD.

William's head had drifted through the class-

room door as it slammed shut behind Lenny. And, from the reaction of the only girl to have noticed, it seemed he'd let his invisibility slip again.

But he couldn't worry too much; he was too excited about the football match to care about anything else. If only he could join in!

He drifted into the boys' loos. As he squeezed himself into a toilet bowl, he imagined himself running down the sports field, the ball at his feet, in the St Sebastian's School strip.

He grimaced as he forced himself round the U-bend and down the pipe that led to the sewer. It was no wonder people fainted when they saw him – he spent his whole time covered in grot!

To take his mind off where he was going, William imagined scoring the winning goal for St Sebastian's and how many friends he'd have then. The whole school would love him!

He dropped out of the end of the pipe into the big, slimy amphitheatre Edith had had built as a place to hold her rants. Sewage pipes sprayed filth round the walls and the whole place was dark, grimy and full of rats.

William didn't mind today, though. He was dreaming of being carried off the school playing field shoulder-high by the rest of the St Sebastian's football team, the crowd cheering his name:

'He ain't very big,

He's skinny like a twig,
But there ain't no one better,
With the bladder of a pig!
Will-i-am! Will-i-am!'

Then his beautiful daydream was cut short by
a wart-covered hand gripping his shoulder.

'Scroggins,' rasped a croaky voice, 'what in the
name of the Black Death are you up to?'

It was Edith Codd – and William was in trouble.
But he didn't care; he had to play in that match!

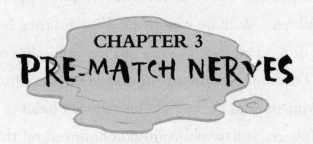

CHAPTER 3
PRE-MATCH NERVES

'WHOAH!'

William launched himself at the severed head flying towards him, but missed it completely. It rolled along the ground, scattering a crowd of rats and coming to a halt in a slimy puddle. It frowned up at William.

'For goodness' sake, William!' the head growled. 'We've been practising all day now. You could have caught that!'

William kicked the head back to its body, which was standing a few metres away with its hands on its hips. He was beginning to regret

asking the Headless Horseman to help him prac-
tise his football skills.

'I just can't get the hang of this goalkeeper
business!' William moaned. 'Why did they have
to go and change the rules of football anyway?'

This time, his friend Ambrose Harbottle took
a run-up and booted the horseman's head at
William. It flew past him and bounced off the
wall of the sewer, landing at his feet.

Ambrose sighed. 'From what I can tell, goalies are meant to *catch* the ball, William,' he said.
'Are you even trying?'

The older ghost noticed that his young friend
seemed upset.

'Look, you'll be fine, lad,' he said, giving the
horseman back his head. 'You can't be any worse
than that Alexander boy they already have in
goal. Now – how about a nice leech break?'

Ambrose had been a leech merchant before
the plague had killed him, and he never went
anywhere without a tin of the wriggling, slimy

slug-like creatures in a pouch on his belt. He pulled a particularly juicy one out and offered it to William.

'Here – have the best one. It'll cheer you up!'

William gagged at the sight of the slimy creature wriggling in Ambrose's scabby hand.

'Erm, it's OK, thanks, Ambrose. I'm fine, really. Listen – thanks for practising with me, you guys. And not a word to Edith, remember!'

The Headless Horseman and Ambrose mimed zipping their lips and slunk off down a nearby tunnel. William headed for a sewage pipe he knew led up to St Sebastian's. Cup final day was here and, rubbish or not, he was desperate to play!

'They're huge!'

'That one's got a scar on his cheek!'

'Why's he holding a baseball bat?'

The whole St Sebastian's football team was

pressed up against the changing-room window, watching the St Mary's team warming up.

'Now I know why no other school would play them!' groaned Matt, the short St Sebastian's right-winger. 'They look like a bunch of deranged gorillas!'

'Oi! That's an insult to gorillas!' complained Lenny, putting on his St Sebastian's shirt. 'That lot look much more dangerous.'

James watched in shock as one of the St Mary's players headbutted the goalpost, snapping it in half. Reg Wharpley, the school caretaker, scurried angrily out on to the pitch with a hammer and nails to fix it.

'Look, we just have to think positive, OK?' said James, turning nervously away from the window.

'Think positive?' cried Ahmed, St Sebastian's central midfielder. 'I'm positively thinking of legging it, if that's what you mean!'

'Plus, we've got that useless nerd Alexander Tick in goal instead of Ben Fletcher!' said Matt.

'We might as well give up now!'

'Leave Alexander alone!' shouted Lenny, giving Matt an evil look. 'He'll be fine!'

'Well, where is he, then?' Matt replied. 'Probably brushing up on some extra maths homework or something.'

The rest of the team laughed, but James and Lenny looked anxiously at each other. Matt was right – where *was* Alexander? Kick-off was in ten minutes, and he was nowhere to be seen.

'Perhaps it's pre-match nerves?' Lenny suggested quietly to James.

'Nah! I reckon his dad's giving him a bit of a team talk . . . You know what Mr Tick's like!' James muttered.

'Uh-oh – speak of the devil!'

Mr Tick had burst into the dressing room. He was wearing a St Sebastian's scarf over his headmaster suit and he had a football rattle poking out of his top pocket.

'Are you ready, boys?' he beamed, punching his

fist in the air. 'It's time to beat St Mary's and show everyone what a great school St Sebastian's is!'

The team looked down at their boots.

'What an old dump it is, more like!' Lenny

muttered to James.

Mr Tick's smile faded, and was replaced by a menacing frown. 'Needless to say,' he boomed, 'any boy who doesn't give one hundred and ten per cent out on that football pitch today will be facing a *long* run of detentions!'

The team groaned.

'In fact!' the headmaster continued, pacing up and down the changing room, 'if you don't go out and beat St Mary's today, you'll *all* be facing detentions – every day for the rest of the month!'

'Great!' James mumbled. 'That's really going to cheer the team up!'

Mr Tick was still in full flow, his face turning red. 'And, yes, that does include you, Alexander!' he roared. His eyes scanned the room, looking for his son.

'Alexander? Are you in here? ALEXAN-DER?' Mr Tick bellowed, looking under a dressing-room bench.

'You, boy!' he said, pointing at James. 'Where is Alexander?'

James shrugged. 'We thought he was with you, sir,' he answered.

Mr Tick turned even redder, flung his scarf over his shoulder, and stormed out of the changing room. They could hear him shouting as he strode out on to the football pitch:

'Remember, boys: you had better win! Or *else*!'

The team sat in silence for a minute after Mr Tick had gone. The only noise was a muffled banging coming from the lost-property cupboard in the corner of the room.

Lenny gave James a nudge. 'What's that noise?' he whispered.

'Who cares?' snapped James, jumping to his feet. 'C'mon, guys – let's get this over with!' He headed for the door.

Lenny caught him up. 'Seriously, James – you don't think Alexander's hiding somewhere do you?' he hissed, as the boys ran out on to the pitch.

'No, I think he's standing over there in the goalmouth. Now shut up and focus on the match!' James replied, grumpily.

Sure enough, there was Alexander, bouncing

a ball up and down next to the goalposts.

'Well, if it isn't our resident brainiac goalie!' Lenny grinned with relief, slapping Alexander on the back.

Alexander turned round to face his friends – but there was something odd about his appearance. In fact, he was looking extremely unwell.

'Blimey, are you OK, Stick?' James asked, jogging up to him. The rest of the team followed.

'Yeah, you look a bit, erm . . . rough!' said Lenny, helpfully.

Alexander didn't reply. He stood clutching the ball with all his might. His skin was stretched and deathly pale. He had big, black bags under his eyes, and his teeth were yellow. Lenny noticed he was thinner, too – and a strong whiff of sewage was coming from his general direction.

'Phwoargh! You absolutely *reek*!' Lenny gasped. 'What have you been doing, cleaning the toilets with your bare hands?'

The goalie shrugged. What looked like a dol-

lop of slime dropped out of his shirt sleeve.

James nudged Lenny. 'Leave him alone, you know how nervous he gets,' he muttered, dragging his friend towards the centre circle. 'Now – let's concentrate on the kick-off!'

As captain of St Sebastian's, James shook hands with the rather large St Mary's captain.

'May the best team win!' he smiled, nervously.

'And may the worse team suffer!' the huge St Mary's captain sneered.

The referee blew the whistle, and the match was under way.

Seconds later, the St Mary's captain was charging full pelt towards Lenny, snarling.

He gulped. This was going to be a long ninety minutes.

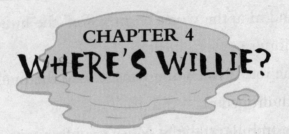

CHAPTER 4
WHERE'S WILLIE?

'Right, you lazy lot!' Edith Codd began, in her horrible screechy voice. 'It's time to fight back!'

The assembled ghosts rolled their eyes and yawned. Edith hadn't stopped ranting about St Sebastian's School since it was built – over one hundred years ago.

'That school is *ruining* our afterlife!' she wailed, pounding her fist on her upturned barrel-cum-ranting-post. 'The noise of all those feet between lessons! The foul sewage they flush down the toilets! It has to stop!'

Ambrose stared into space and slipped another

leech into his mouth. He, along with most of the other spirits, found Edith's constant ravings more annoying than the noise from the school. But over time he'd learnt it was best to go along with her plans if you wanted to get any peace in the sewer.

'This used to be a respectable mass grave!' Edith droned on. 'And *now* look at it!'

Bertram Ruttle, the sewer's resident musician, dozed off at the front, his grip loosening on the bone xylophone he was holding. A cheeky young ghost next to him slid it out slowly from between his fingers. Ambrose yawned for the tenth time. When was the old hag going to shut up?

'We need a plan!' Edith bellowed, trying to rouse the assembled crowd into some kind of action. 'We need a gruesome scheme to drive the pupils out of St Sebastian's School!'

At that moment, Bertram woke up and realised his instrument was missing.

'Oi!' he yelled over Edith's drone. 'Who's stolen my xylophone?'

'Shut up!' grumbled the Headless Horseman. 'Some of us are trying to sleep over here!'

Edith tutted. 'Is no one listening? WE NEED TO GET RID OF THOSE PESKY SHOOLCHILDREN!' she screamed.

Bertram threw one of his xylophone beaters at the young ghost in revenge. The boy caught it and chucked it at the horseman.

Bertram got up and barged through the crowd to retrieve his property, and within minutes, the whole amphitheatre was in uproar.

Ambrose seized the opportunity to slink off without being noticed.

But before he could settle down quietly with his beloved leech stash, he felt a foul stench waft over his shoulder. Edith had found him.

'I couldn't help noticing that young William wasn't at my anti-St Sebastian's meeting,' she croaked, suspiciously. 'You haven't seen him, have you, Ambrose?'

He gulped.

'W-William?' the old ghost mumbled, trying to look innocent. 'N-no, I haven't seen him, Edith.'

The hag moved in a little closer. 'Are you sure about that?' she hissed.

'Would I lie to you, Edith?' he laughed, nervously. 'Now – can I tempt you with a leech?'

Edith's eyes glowed red as she grabbed Ambrose's leech tin with a flaky hand and gave it a shake.

'You know how much you love your leeches?' the old hag snarled.

He nodded.

'Well, wouldn't it be a *shame* if someone set them all *free* one night?' Edith leered.

'Edith!' Ambrose cried. 'You wouldn't!'

She gave him a sickly smile. 'Oh, wouldn't I? Unless, of course, you help me find William. I'm sure he's up to no good!'

Ambrose sighed. Why was he always getting dragged into the silly bat's schemes? All he wanted was an easy life, and he hadn't had a moment's peace since he died!

'Well,' he groaned, realising that Edith had won again, 'I suppose he *might* be up at the school . . .'

The hag grabbed Ambrose's wrist. 'Come on, let's go!' she said. 'And if I discover he's helping that pesky school out, there'll be big trouble!'

Ambrose sighed heavily. *Here we go again!* he thought . . .

William was having a brilliant time, and no one seemed to have noticed he wasn't the team's real goalkeeper yet.

'Oi! Alexander! That was rubbish!' Matt yelled in his face. 'You couldn't catch a cold!'

William's only problem was the game itself. He just couldn't seem to stop the ball, or wrestle it off the giant St Mary's boys. He'd let in five goals already and his own teammates were giving him evil looks.

'Alexander! Pay attention!' Lenny yelled, his hands on his hips. 'We're losing here, you know!'

William picked the ball out of the net again. He tried to ignore the insults; at least he had some real, live teammates, even if they did think he was rubbish.

If this works, maybe I could go to some lessons as Alexander, too! he thought to himself, smiling. *I could play in the team every week, and hang out with James and Lenny!*

A horribly familiar voice woke him from his daydream.

'Scroggins!' it rasped. 'I might have known!'

William's blood – if he'd had any – would have frozen solid.

'Edith!' he groaned. 'How did you find me?'

The old hag cackled. She'd turned herself invisible and was standing behind the William in goal. He was so distressed he let his Alexander disguise flicker for a moment. The ball flew right through his stomach and into the goal.

'ALEXANDER!' James bellowed, glaring at him. 'Get a grip!'

William turned back to where Edith's voice was coming from.

'I'm not doing any harm!' he hissed out of the

corner of his mouth. 'I just want to play football!'

'And I suppose helping the St Sebastian's football team isn't doing any harm?' Edith growled.

William groaned as another shot flew past him into the goal. This time, the ball went straight through his arm. The St Mary's striker did a victory dance on the touchline to celebrate.

'I don't think I'm really helping them, Edith!' he sighed. 'I'm useless!'

'Well, put your uselessness to some *use* then, you traitor!' the invisible voice growled. 'Do something nasty. Play by medieval rules, for a start!'

William looked upfield. St Sebastian's had a free kick. He didn't get this modern type of football. In his day, it wasn't a game unless you managed to kick at least three people in the head and, ideally, broke someone's leg, too. But in this match, every time someone tripped up an opponent, they stopped play and had a so-called 'free kick'!

'You heard me!' Edith shouted at him. 'Play rough! Cause some damage!'

William was tempted. He was useless in goal, and useless at modern football. Maybe if he showed off some medieval skills, the St Sebastian's boys would like him more.

'I want to see blood on the pitch!' screamed Edith. 'I want pupils running for their lives!'

William sighed. He'd heard boys in St Sebastian's tell each other they needed 'chill pills' when they were wound up. Perhaps he could get Edith one after the game?

Ambrose pumped his fist in the air.

'Come on, St Sebastian's! You can do it!' he yelled, willing James to score.

The spectators around him looked about, terrified. Where had that voice come from? And what was that smell?

Some of the mums and dads shuffled away from the bodiless voice, mumbling to each other.

'Something odd going on!'

'Smells like sewage!'

'What's that crunching noise?'

But Ambrose didn't care. He was wondering if he could get away with coming every week.

CHAPTER 5
WHO'S IN GHOUL?

'FROAAAARGH!'

James groaned as a size-eleven St Mary's football boot slammed his head into the grass. He looked up to see the huge, shaven-headed defender stride off with the ball, and was still picking bits of grass out of his teeth when the opposing team floated another easy goal past Alexander.

'C'mon, guys, it's only eight–nil!' cried Lenny, giving James a hand up. 'We can't let them beat us!'

Ahmed limped up to the centre circle and gave Lenny an evil look. He had stud impressions on his forehead, and blood trickling down his arm from what looked like a bite mark.

'We're not getting beaten, Lenny,' he grumbled. 'We're getting beaten *up*!'

James did a quick survey of the St Sebastian's team before kicking off again. They certainly were a sorry state: covered in bruises, eight–nil

down and nothing to look forward to after the game except for a long run of detentions with Mr Tick. Could the cup final get any worse?

'BLEEEURGH!'

Within seconds, James was face down on the grass again.

'This is worse than school dinners!' he muttered to himself, as he watched the St Mary's winger's back disappear down the pitch.

William adjusted his gloves and turned back to the game. Edith had gone off to shout at Ambrose, so he had a couple of minutes to decide what to do. Should he show them how good he was at medie-val-style football? Or should he just stick it out in goal?

The ball flew towards him. He tried to catch it, but his disguise flickered and the ball flew straight through him.

As he went to pick up the ball, a dollop of slime fell out of his shorts. William looked round quickly; it didn't look like anyone had noticed.

'Blast!' he muttered to himself. 'I thought I scraped all that off before the match!'

What he really needed to do, he decided, was concentrate on his 'Alexander' disguise. If anyone caught a glimpse of the real William, they'd never let him stay in the team . . .

'Alexander, that was your most useless effort yet!' Matt screamed from the halfway line, stamping his foot.

'Come on, guys – let's play as a team! No more arguing!' James cried, giving Matt a stern look.

Matt did have a point, though: Alexander was being particularly rubbish, even for someone who was allergic to sport. The ball seemed to float right through him whenever he tried to catch it.

And instead of concentrating on the game, he kept shouting and gesturing at the empty goal net behind him.

'I *knew* it!' said Lenny, jogging alongside James. 'He's finally cracked. I told him all that science homework was bad for the brain!'

James gave Lenny a shove. 'Well, you should be totally safe then. You've never done any in your life!'

'That's what I'm worried about!' cried Lenny. 'If Stick's lost his marbles, who am I going to copy mine off?'

'OOOOARGH!'

James didn't have a chance to reply before a flying St Mary's fist sent him crashing face down into the turf. A boot hoofed him in the ribs for good measure while he lay there.

As he gingerly stood up, another shot flew towards their goalkeeper. Alexander moved to meet it this time, but seemed to vanish into thin air just before the ball hit him.

James blinked and rubbed his eyes. There was Alexander picking the ball out of the net. Maybe James was going mad himself . . .

'Ten–nil!'

'There's only one St Mary's!'

'Here we go, here we go, here we go!'

James trudged past the jubilant St Mary's fans to the centre circle to kick off yet again. *Surely* it must be half-time by *now*?

Sighing, he tucked in his shirt and rolled the ball to Matt.

Matt, caked head to toe in mud, barely had the energy to pass the ball back to James. He turned round to switch the play to Ahmed, but their winger was lying on the floor, groaning. A large St Mary's player was wiping his knuckles nearby.

'Oi! Ref!' yelled James. 'This is getting out of hand!'

But the referee was standing frozen to the spot, staring at Alexander. The St Sebastian's goalkeeper was talking to the empty net again, and kept flickering in and out of view like a bad TV signal.

James poked the referee in the ribs.

'Er, ref!' he said, catching Lenny's eye. 'I think it might be half-time!'

More importantly, it was time they had a quick chat with Alexander. The referee blew his whistle, looking rather shaken. 'R-right! Yes! H-half-time, everybody!' he shouted, in a rather quavery voice.

As the two teams trudged back to the changing rooms, James and Lenny grabbed one of Alexander's arms each and marched him round the back of the goal.

'Alexander! What's *wrong* with you?' cried Lenny, shaking him. 'You're costing us the match!'

Alexander just stood there, staring at Lenny. His eyes had gone a dark black colour and the horrible smell was getting worse.

'Alexander! I'm asking you a question!' Lenny repeated, shaking him again.

James just stared quietly at the goalkeeper.

He put his hand on Lenny's shoulder.

'Um . . . Lenny, can I have a quick word, please?' he hissed, looking closely at Alexander's face.

Lenny ignored him. 'And another thing! That free kick you let in – it was absolutely . . . absolutely . . . erm . . .'

But he couldn't finish his sentence. He tailed off and started staring too. Alexander was as white as a sheet and kept vanishing into thin air for a split second at a time. He didn't say a word, but whenever he opened his mouth, a row of yellow, rotting stumps appeared instead of teeth.

'Yuck! Alexander! What the . . .?'

Lenny dropped Alexander's arm. Even through the goalie glove, he could feel it was ice cold. As the arm dropped to Alexander's side, a thick dollop of slime oozed out of the sleeve and fell on the ground.

'Lenny. A word. *Now*!' James hissed.

But Lenny stood rooted to the spot, petrified.

Alexander stared back at him without moving
or blinking. What looked like a maggot emerged
from his ear and crawled round on to his face.

'Lenny! NOW!' James hissed, grabbing his
friend by the shirt and dragging him towards the
changing room.

'We won't be a minute, Alexander!' he called
over his shoulder, giving the goalkeeper a nervous

smile. 'Just going to talk tactics!'

James heaved Lenny along by the arm. His friend made no effort to walk on his own. He was quivering, mouth open, pointing at Alexander.

'A-A-Alexander!' he gasped under his breath. 'He's a g-g-ghost!'

James nodded. As he bundled Lenny through the changing-room door, Alexander lurched back towards his goal and started talking to the empty net again.

The second half could well be worse than they feared.

CHAPTER 6
HALF-SLIME

James splashed a handful of ice-cold water over Lenny's face.

'Blurgh!' Lenny howled. 'What was *that* for?'

'To bring you round!' James cried. 'You're hysterical!'

'Are you surprised?' Lenny hissed in a frenzied whisper. 'Our best friend has been turned into some kind of spook! We saw it with our own eyes! He kept vanishing!'

Lenny started shaking again, and tried to wriggle free of James's grip.

James gave him a hard slap in the face.

'OOWWWWW!'

'Pull yourself together, man!' said his friend, holding Lenny by the shoulders. 'Alexander needs our help!'

Lenny went even paler. 'Alexander!' he cried, clutching his head in his hands. 'What have they *done* to him! The poor thing!'

James lifted his hand ready to slap again.

'I know he was a bit of a nerd,' Lenny wailed, 'but he was a good friend! And he always helped us with our science homework! OOWWWWW!'

This time, James's slap seemed to have done the trick. Lenny shook his head, took a deep breath, and turned to him.

'Now what are we going to do?' he said. 'We need a plan!'

James raised his hand to dish out another slap.

'You sure you don't need another one, Lenny?' he smirked. 'I enjoyed that!'

Lenny drew himself up to his full height and looked down at James.

53

'Just try it, matey!' he warned.

'Well, first things first,' James said, quickly dropping his hand. 'We need to find out what they've done with the real Alexander. And then . . .'

Suddenly, their conversation was cut short by the sound of someone crashing through the changing-room door. Mr Tick stalked into the room.

'What, in the name of St Sebastian, do you call *that*?' he demanded. His nostrils flared in and out like he was about to breathe fire, and a single bead of sweat rolled down his forehead.

'You, boy!' he roared, pointing to Ahmed. 'Tell me what you're all playing at!'

The headmaster stared at Ahmed, who was bandaging up his leg with an old sock. He pounded on the door of the lost-property cupboard as if to hurry a response out of him.

'Whimper!'

James and Lenny looked at the cupboard and then at each other; what was that noise?

'Um, th-th-they were rather b-b-big, s-s-sir!'

Ahmed stuttered, shuffling from foot to foot.

Mr Tick's eyes started to bulge out of his head like gobstoppers.

'Rather big?' he shouted. 'Rather *big*? What kind of excuse is *that*?'

He gave the dented door another punch.

BOOM!

'Whimper!'

James and Lenny nodded at each other. This time there was definitely a noise from the cupboard's general direction.

Mr Tick, meanwhile, looked like he was trying to stop himself from exploding. He was taking deep breaths and holding his hands behind his back. When he finally spoke it was in a low voice, shaking with rage.

'Now, listen here, you boys,' he growled. The team all gulped at once. 'I don't care if the score is ten–nil. It could be a *hundred*–nil for all I care. I want you to win. I *expect* you to win. And if you don't win, you will *all* face the consequences. Including you, Alexander!'

The headmaster scanned the room for his son.

'ALEXANDER?' he shouted. 'Where is that useless boy?'

James cleared his throat. 'I think he's getting in some extra practice, sir!' he replied, pointing out of the dressing-room window.

In the distance, the ghostly Alexander was pacing about in his goal with jerky movements, bits of slime dropping from his arms.

'Well,' Mr Tick harrumphed, 'he certainly needs it!'

And with that, he stormed out, slamming the door behind him.

As the team limped reluctantly back out for the second half, James and Lenny approached the dented cupboard door Mr Tick had been pounding.

James knocked on it, nervously.

'Er, hello?' he said. 'Is there anyone in there?'

A muffled groan came from inside. 'Go away!'

a faint voice cried. 'Please leave me alone!'

Lenny gave the cupboard a shake. 'Alexander!' he shouted. 'Is that you? Are you safe?'

'Lenny! James!' the muffled voice said, sounding relieved. 'Get me out of here! Some monster has been pounding the door in, and I don't think this two-millimetre-thick aluminium alloy will withstand the strain for much longer!'

James and Lenny laughed. It was Alexander all right!

James glanced around the changing room and found a rusty javelin under one of the benches. He stuck the pointy end in the cupboard's keyhole and, with a sharp jerk, snapped the door open. Lenny peered in.

'About time!' the muffled voice moaned. 'What took you so long?'

At the bottom of the cupboard was a pile of smelly football shirts, old boots and some suspiciously stained-looking shorts. The pile wriggled about for a second before Alexander's head poked out the top.

'Alexander! You're safe!' Lenny cried. 'Thank goodness!'

Alexander frowned.

'Oh, right. You must have been really worried to come and rescue me after a mere *hour*!' he said, sarcastically. 'Now, what moron locked me in here? I may be rubbish in goal, but there was no need for that!'

'I don't think it was one of the team, Stick,' Lenny said. 'There's something scarier than St Mary's out on the pitch this afternoon!'

Alexander was trying to scramble out of the narrow cupboard without much success. 'Scarier than St Mary's?' he muttered. 'What can be worse than those bruising bullies?'

James stuck out a hand to help Alexander.

'A ghost!' Lenny replied with a shiver. 'We've got a ghost on our team, and it's up to no good!'

Alexander rolled his eyes. 'I see!' he grumbled. 'Not only do I get bundled into a smelly cupboard

and shut in the dark for an hour — now my own
friends are taking the mickey!'

Lenny shook his head. 'No, there really is,
Stick, I swear! And he looks even weirder than

you!'

'Come on, let's face it, Alexander – it wouldn't be the first time something strange had happened round here, would it?' James added.

Alexander frowned. 'A *ghost*?' he cried. 'That's what locked me in here?'

Lenny nodded.

'Wow!' Alexander gasped. 'That *is* scarier than St Mary's!'

James raised his eyebrows as though he'd just had a brainwave.

'Scarier than St Mary's!' he mumbled to himself. 'I wonder . . . That just might work!'

He stopped helping Alexander out of the cupboard, grabbed him by the collar and flung him back into the pile of mucky sports gear.

'*Ow!*' Alexander wailed. 'What was *that* for?'

Lenny whirled round and shot James an evil look. 'James!' he grunted. '*I'm* gonna start dishing out slaps in a minute. This is no time for jokes!'

A smile was playing round the corners of James's mouth. He slammed the cupboard door shut on Alexander and quickly wedged a chair in front of it.

'Lemme out, you idiots!' Alexander screeched, pounding the inside of the door. 'Have you lost your minds?'

James grabbed Lenny by the arm and dragged him towards the changing-room door.

'Is this supposed to be funny, James?' said Lenny, trying to wriggle free of his grasp. 'Or have you been possessed, too? We can't leave Alexander in there! And what about the ghost?'

James pushed him out on to the pitch and started striding towards the centre circle.

'You know what, Lenny?' he said, purposefully. 'We might just *need* something scarier than St Mary's if we're going to win this match!'

Lenny sighed. As if it wasn't enough having a supernatural being in goal, now his only ally had totally lost the plot.

James grabbed the ball and stuck it on the centre circle with a big grin. 'Right, lads!' he bellowed at the whole team. 'Follow my lead!'

He looked over his shoulder at Lenny. 'Don't worry, mate!' he hissed. 'I've got a plan!'

CHAPTER 7
OWN GHOUL

James smirked and looked over his shoulder at the ghostly St Sebastian's keeper.

'So, you wanna play football do you?' he muttered under his breath. 'Well, I'll show you *football*!'

Matt rolled him the ball from kick-off, and he trapped it neatly. A St Mary's player stood in front of him, menacingly waving a football boot over his head. But instead of dribbling round him, James turned on his heel and started running towards the St Sebastian's goal.

'Let's see if *this* wakes you up!' he cried, picking up speed.

Lenny looked on in surprise.

'Get with it, James!' he yelled. 'We changed ends, remember?'

James ignored him and carried on sprinting towards his own goal. Lenny sighed and wondered what he had done to deserve such stupid friends.

'Wakey, wakey, James!' he cried. 'You're going the WRONG WAY!'

James showed no sign of slowing down as he reached the penalty area, so Lenny took matters into his own hands.

'You'll thank me for this, mate!' he cried, and launched himself into a sliding tackle right behind the sprinting James – who had clearly lost the plot thanks to this whole ghost goalie problem.

But James saw him coming, and jumped his tackle neatly. Lenny looked on aghast as James aimed, then took a powerful shot at his own goal.

'Take *that*!' he cried, as he booted the ball with all his might. 'Now, let's see what happens!'

As the ball swerved through the air, the ghostly keeper moved across to try and save it. There was no way a goalie that rubbish could save a shot like that, the horrified St Sebastian's team thought.

Or was there?

What a strange game this modern football is! William thought to himself, surprised. *In medieval times, you only tried to score in your opponent's goal. But James is charging towards me like he wants to score in his own net!*

He smacked his goalie gloves together and jumped up and down. 'Come on, William!' he said to himself. 'You can do it! You can do it!'

He was determined to put on a better performance this half. None of the St Sebastian's pupils would like him if he kept letting in easy goals – and William was desperate to be one of the gang. If that meant playing medieval style, then so be it.

'Come on, William!' he repeated. 'You can save this!'

He was even more surprised when Lenny tried to tackle James. Members of the same team tackling each other? Things were much simpler in the 1340s!

As James's shot curled towards the goal, William took two steps forwards and flung himself at it with all his might. His light, spectral body drifted through the air like a feather.

'Yesss!' he cried, folding his arms round the ball and landing in the mud. 'I did it!'

He picked himself up, kept a tight hold of the ball, and looked straight down the middle of the pitch at the bemused St Mary's team.

'This is it!' William said to himself. 'This is my chance!'

He took a deep breath, tucked the ball under his arm, and started to run. He was going to show everybody what he was made of; he was going to win the match for St Sebastian's!

Lenny and the rest of the team breathed a sigh of relief as their goalkeeper saved James's shot. Lenny jogged over to his friend and grabbed him by the shirt.

'James!' he hissed. 'What the hell are you doing? You nearly just scored the worst own-goal ever!'

James smiled at him.

'All part of the plan!' he smirked.

Lenny snorted. 'And what plan is that?' he muttered. 'The lose-by-even-more-than-we-are-now plan? The force-the-dangerous-ghost-into-killing-us-all plan?

'That's just it!' James cried, slapping Lenny on the back. 'I'm trying to provoke the ghost into getting angry!' he continued, quietly.

Lenny shook his head in disbelief. 'Perfect. We've got a phantom on the pitch that might kill us all any second, and *you've* decided to wind it up.'

James nodded again.

'Brilliant, isn't it?' James smiled. 'If he gets angry enough, he could take out the whole St Mary's team!'

Lenny stared aghast at his friend.

'Or it could take out the whole St Sebastian's team!' he cried. 'Or the whole football match, for that matter. Or everyone in the school. Or the whole town! Did you think of that, James? Did that even cross your mind for a second?'

James shook his head. 'Oh, spare me the hysterics!' he said. 'He joined our team, didn't he? He must like us! Look – he's all fired up already!'

Lenny whirled round and stared at the ghostly goalkeeper. He certainly seemed to have livened up a bit. His eyes were glowing bright red instead of black, and he was clutching the ball and pawing his foot on the ground like a bull preparing to charge.

'You'd better be right, James!' Lenny whispered. 'Or this could turn nasty!'

But James didn't answer. He was watching with glee as their team's ghostly goalie charged out of the penalty area, still holding the ball.

Ambrose spat out the leech he was eating and jumped up and down. At last, William was getting into the game!

'Go on, William!' he roared. 'You show 'em!'

A big smile spread over his face as William began to sprint down the pitch with the ball under his arm.

'OOOARGH!'

A St Mary's player tried to get in his way, but William jabbed a finger in the boy's eye.

'That's it!' Ambrose cried. 'Do it medieval style! Show the wimps how to play *real* football!'

'Yuck! Mumph!'

Another St Mary's player tried to tackle him,

but William flung a stinking dollop of sewer slime right at his face. The defender doubled over, clutching his mouth.

'Arrrgh! That tastes gross!' he spat.

'Go on!' Ambrose yelled. 'Get another one!'

By now, William's eyes were glowing bright red, and slime poured out in a stream behind him as he ran, spattering any players he passed. He let out a grating, ghostly scream.

'Go on, lad!' cried Ambrose. 'Put it in the net!'

The big St Mary's keeper froze with fear as this terrifying sight stampeded towards him.
He took two steps backwards, tripped over and curled in a ball, whimpering.

'Don't hurt me!' he mumbled, as William leapt over him. 'Mummy!'

William didn't even notice. He dug his heels into the turf, came to a skidding halt and, with a final, piercing screech, hurled the ball into the back of the net.

'GOOOAAAAL!' Ambrose screamed.

'Yessssss!'

Everyone else on the pitch and the touchlines was completely silent. The St Sebastian's team members all had their mouths open in shock.

'W-w-what was t-t-that?' Ahmed wailed after a minute's silence.

'D-d-d-dunno!' Matt replied, rubbing his eyes.

The referee was white as a sheet and shaking with fright. He put his whistle to his lips with trembling hands.

PHEEEEEEEEEEEP!

'G-g-goal!' he stuttered. Never mind the hand-ball and horrendous fouls; he didn't want that crazed St Sebastian's goalie turning on *him* next!

James smiled and gave the terrified Lenny a slap on the back.

'See!' he said. 'Ten–one! We're back in the game!'

Lenny gulped. The St Mary's players were looking furious and punching their fists into their hands.

'I hope you're ready for some carnage, James!' he growled. 'Cos I think this is about to turn nasty. Very nasty indeed.'

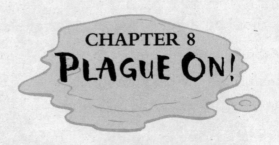

CHAPTER 8
PLAGUE ON!

Ambrose's goal celebrations came to a sudden halt as he got a sharp kick in the shin from an invisible foot.

'Ow!' he cried. 'What was *that* for?'

'Stop cheering at once, you idiot!' Edith squawked, giving him another kick. 'You'll only encourage the boy!'

Ambrose stopped clapping. 'Well, it was a good goal,' he muttered. 'Why are you so angry with William anyway?'

Edith was almost beside herself with rage. 'Why am I angry?' she screeched. 'WHY AM I

ANGRY?'

Here we go, Ambrose thought, *another rant* . . .

Edith poked him in the ribs. 'I'm *angry* because that boy should be scaring the St Sebastian's players off. Instead, he's just scored a goal for them. He's not fighting them, he's HELPING THEM OUT!'

Edith paused for breath. If she hadn't been invisible at that moment, her flaky white face would have been bright red with anger.

'Now, come on, Ambrose,' she hissed. 'Let's get out there and cause some trouble. This is a great opportunity to do away with that horrible school!'

But Ambrose wasn't paying attention. He was shouting instructions to William.

'Get those St Mary's bullies!' he roared. 'Poke their eyes out!'

Edith stamped her rotten, magotty foot. 'Right! That's it!' she cried. 'I'm surrounded by traitors!'

Ambrose ignored her. 'Come on, James!' he

yelled, following the game. 'Put some effort in!'

Edith gave him one last jab in the ribs.

'Well, if you won't help me, I'll find someone who will!' she croaked. 'And when we finally get rid of this ghastly school, it'll be no thanks to *you*!'

Down the touchline, a group of mums and dads were cowering together, looking around them frantically.

'Where *is* that awful voice coming from?' whispered one.

'Search me!' said another.

'I dunno about you two,' a third parent shuddered, 'but this game's giving me the c-c-creeps!'

Back in the sewer, Edith stormed into the amphitheatre. 'Oi! You two!' she screeched. 'Come with me – *now*!'

In a corner of the amphitheatre, Bertram Ruttle was picking out a medieval tune on his bone xylophone. The Headless Horseman was nodding along in time, as Bertram used his leg-bone beaters to bash out the chorus.

Both ghosts looked up as Edith stormed in.

'What is it, Edith?' said Bertram, dropping his xylophone, guiltily. Some of the ribs it was constructed from were Edith's, and he'd taken them without asking.

'That boy William is causing havoc up there!' she complained. 'He's helping the St Sebastian's football team to win. We have to stop him!'

The Headless Horseman's ears pricked up at the mention of football. He scooped up his head and turned it towards Edith.

'He's playing football, you say?' he asked, excited. 'What's the score? How's he doing?'

Edith slapped her forehead with her hand. A worm dropped out of her wiry red hair. 'Never mind what the score is!' she cried. 'He's missing a great opportunity to get rid of St Sebastian's!'

'Yeah, yeah,' said Bertram, 'but has he scored?'

'YES!' screeched Edith. 'That's the whole *point*! He's scored *for* St Sebastian's, not *against* them! That's why I need you two; we're going to go up there, join the St Mary's team, and cause some serious damage to St Sebastian's!'

The Headless Horseman and Bertram jumped up and ran towards the sewage pipe that led to the school. William had scored! Good for him!

Edith smiled as the two ghosts squeezed themselves up a sludgy, stinky pipe.

'At last!' she said to herself. 'Some ghosts who are willing to join my campaign!'

The Headless Horseman and Bertram sprinted from the boys' toilet block to the sports field, turning themselves invisible as they went.

'This is gonna be *great*!' cried Bertram. 'I love

a game of footy!'

They found Ambrose on the touchline by following the sound of crunching leeches.

'What's the score?' asked the Headless Horseman.

Ambrose sighed. 'St Sebastian's are ten–one down; William's just scored, but they'll need another nine goals to even draw!'

The horseman started doing some leg stretches.

'Looks like they could use an extra player or two then, eh, Bertram?' he cried.

But Bertram was already on the pitch.

'William! William!' he called out to the St Sebastian's keeper, who had just made another good save. 'Roll me the ball!'

The rest of the team looked around, confused.

'W-where are all these voices coming from?' Ahmed wailed.

'Not from inside my head then!' said Lenny, looking somewhat relieved.

William smiled and rolled the ball out in the direction of Bertram's voice. Lenny looked on in

shock as the ball stopped, flicked itself into the air,
and began to charge down the pitch on its own.

'Is the b–b–ball haunted now, too?' he whispered
to James. 'Can we just stop this before we all get
killed, please?'

James smiled as a St Mary's player tried to block it. It swerved to the left, then to the right, and carried on down the wing. Another player tried to smother it like a rugby ball, but it flew up in the air, bashed him on the head, and carried on rolling fast towards the St Mary's goal.

While the rest of the team stared in shock, James sprang into action. He sprinted down the middle of the pitch at full pelt.

'In the middle!' cried James, waving at thin air. 'I'm unmarked!'

The ball stopped dead, jumped a little, then flew over the penalty area in a perfect cross.

'Good ball!' shouted James, jumping high in the air and heading it into the goal. 'Yessssss!'

He reeled away, his shirt over his head. 'Ten–two!' he whooped. 'What a goal!'

But the rest of the pitch was silent. Every single player on both teams was absolutely terrified. Rooted to the spot. A huge St Mary's midfielder started to cry.

As the ball floated back to the centre circle,
Lenny nudged James.

'This is too weird!' he growled. 'There's more
than one ghost at work here! Let's leg it!'

But James shrugged him off. 'Nonsense!' he

said. 'We can win this! Look – they're terrified!'

The St Mary's team was nervously huddled in its own half, gesturing at its team minibus.

'OI, REF! BLOW THE WHISTLE! LET'S KICK OFF!' James yelled.

The frightened referee fumbled for his whistle and gave a weak 'tooooooooooot'.

'Come on, team!' James shouted. 'Let's go!

Edith arrived on the touchline just in time to see an invisible Bertram run down the wing, the horseman trip up a St Mary's defender, and James score St Sebastian's second goal.

'WHAAAAAAAAT?' she wailed. '*More* traitors?'

She flung a dollop of sewage in Bertram's general direction. 'You're helping St Sebastian's, too?' she screeched. 'Is there *no one* I can trust? You should be ashamed to call yourselves ghosts!'

Bertram ignored her and took up his favourite

position on the wing.

'That's *it*!' Edith growled, furiously. She pushed up her grimy sleeves, checked that she couldn't be seen, and charged out on to the pitch. 'If you want a job done,' she muttered, 'do it yourself!'

She stood next to the St Mary's captain, who was chewing his fingernails and whimpering into his football shirt.

'Watch out, St Sebastian's!' she cried. 'You're finally going to get what you deserve!'

The St Mary's captain looked around wildly and dropped the ball on to the centre spot.

'W-w-who said that?' he sobbed, wrinkling up his nose. 'And why can I smell cowpats?'

CHAPTER 9
THAT'S THE SPIRIT

'Sh-sh-shall we kick off again, ref?' the St
Mary's captain wobbled.

The referee timidly blew his whistle again.
'Do what you like!' he whimpered. 'I don't
know *what's* going on!'

The St Mary's captain shrugged and passed
the ball to a teammate, who started running nervously down the wing, looking around the pitch
with wide, frightened eyes.

'Here we go again, Bertram!' cried the Headless Horseman.

Bertram pulled his invisible socks up, broke

into a run, and charged into the St Mary's player
with all his might. The boy went flying.

'Oooof!' he groaned, crashing into the mud. He
looked wildly about him. 'Who did that? Where
are you?' he shouted, swiping at the air around
him. 'I know you're there! Lemme see you!'

Bertram laughed and rolled the ball gently back
to William in goal. 'Come on, William!' he cried.
'Time for another Scroggins Special, I think!'

William grinned, dropped the ball at his feet,
and dribbled out of his area.

'Go on . . . er . . . whoever you are!' cried
James.

William nodded and charged forwards. His
eyes glowed bright red again and some ectoplasm
foamed out of his mouth and on to his chin. He
couldn't help it; this was so exciting!

In front of him, a St Mary's midfielder's shorts
suddenly pulled themselves down, revealing a
pair of pink frilly pants.

'Argh! They're my sister's, honest!' he whimpered.

'Thanks, Bertram!' cried William, continuing to run.

Another St Mary's player screamed as his football shirt lifted itself up and covered his eyes.

'Who switched out the lights?'

'Cheers, horseman!' William shouted over his shoulder.

But as he approached the St Mary's penalty area, he felt a familiar chill on the back of his neck.

'William Scroggins!' Edith's voice rasped. 'You'll pay for this!'

William shivered, but kept right on running.

'Give me the ball, NOW, Scroggins!' Edith screamed, bearing down on him, her voice getting screechier. 'Or else I'll – EEEEARGH!'

'Go, William! You can do it!' shouted the Headless Horseman. He must have tripped the old hag up!

William was clean through on goal. This was

it! The St Mary's goalkeeper took one look at his red eyes, pale face and foaming mouth and fled from the pitch in terror.

'Mummy!' he blubbered, 'Mummy! Get me out of here! I want my blankie!'

William smiled, trapped the ball, and tapped it into the open goal. This was brilliant; St Sebastian's were catching up, and it was all thanks to him and his ghostly friends!

As he jogged back to his own half, James ran up and slapped William on the back. 'Good goal, mate!' he said. 'Let's get another!'

William said nothing, but gave James a big, toothy grin. *I'm one of the team!* he thought, feeling all warm inside.

James shuddered at the sight of the rotting stumps in William's mouth. He caught Lenny's eye.

'Wherever that kid's from, they don't have dentists!' he joked.

But Lenny was much too terrified to laugh.

'Wherever that kid comes from, we should *not* be playing football with him!' Lenny replied with a shudder.

Within seconds of kick-off, Bertram had picked up the ball again and was making yet another invisible attack. This time, however, no one from St Mary's stood in his way. Instead, they tumbled over each other to get out of the path of the ghostly ball.

'It's coming towards us!'

'Don't try and stop it!'

'Aaaargh! Gemme outta here!'

They scattered in all directions, fleeing from the pitch and heading for their minibus in the car park. Bertram just shrugged.

'This is too easy!' he called over to the Headless Horseman, who was following some of the St Mary's players and making silly ghost noises. 'I could do with a bit of a challenge!'

He rolled the ball into the empty net.

'Yesss!' James cheered, punching the air.

'Thanks, wherever you are!'

Meanwhile, the Headless Horseman turned his attention to the last three St Mary's players on the pitch. As they placed the ball on the centre circle to kick off, he floated over and switched the ball for his head, making it visible at the same time.

One St Mary's player kicked it to another without looking.

'EAAAAURGH!' his teammate cried, looking at his feet. 'What the . . . What on earth . . . AAAAAAAARGH!'

The horseman's head looked up at him and laughed.

'Ha, ha!' he leered, trying to bite the boy's football boot. 'Gotcha! You should have seen your face!'

With that, the last of the St Mary's team ran screaming off the pitch, waving their arms in the

air. A furious, invisible Edith howled after them as they sprinted towards their minibus.

'Cowards!' she screeched. 'Come back here!'

The St Mary's players just sprinted even faster. They were followed by an equally horrified group of parents and teachers.

'Aaaaaaaargh! Leg it!' one cried.

'Faster! The voice is following us!'

'To the bus, quick!'

'I'm definitely complaining to the PTA!'

Edith turned round, caught her breath and furiously stomped back towards the football pitch. She could see James and William scoring repeatedly in the empty St Mary's goal.

'Betrayed by my own ghosts!' she grumbled. 'Well, it'll take more than that to stop Edith

Codd.'

'Ten all!' Ambrose cried excitedly from the touchline. 'Good one, James! Good one, Bertram!'

'Oh, shut up, Ambrose!' Edith snorted. 'St Sebastian's haven't won yet, you know!'

Ambrose was still invisible, but she could tell he was doing a dance of some description. The grass all around him kept flattening itself as he shifted his feet about.

'Oh, give up, Edith!' he whooped. 'They've almost done it! St Sebastian's only need one more goal to win, and St Mary's have scarpered!'

Edith strode down the pitch, fuming. 'St Mary's may indeed have run off,' she croaked, menacingly. 'But Edith Codd is still very much here. And St Sebastian's hasn't seen anything yet!'

CHAPTER 10
ODD 'N' TRIPS

The Headless Horseman ran in a circle, whooping.

'We're gonna win! We're gonna win!' he cried.

James laughed, spinning round to follow the invisible voice.

'Yeah!' James cried. 'Now stand still, wherever you are – you're making me dizzy!'

On the other side of the pitch, the equally invisible Bertram was charging along with the ball. But instead of shooting into the deserted St Mary's goal as James had expected, the ball stopped dead, rolled backwards, then started drifting straight towards him.

'Owww!' moaned Bertram, picking himself up. He'd felt someone tackle him hard. 'Who did that? Gimme the ball back!'

There was no one to be seen, but a cackle and a terrible whiff told him all he needed to know: Edith was back on the pitch. And she was running straight at James, the ball at her feet.

'I'll show him!' she grunted. 'Thinks he can defeat Edith Codd, does he?'

James was still laughing, trying to grab the invisible horseman as he ran about.

'You won't be laughing in a minute, you disgusting pupil!' Edith cackled, drawing her foot back to shoot. 'Take *this*!'

She booted the ball as hard as she could at James's head, screeching with laughter.

It hit him on the back of the head and bounced off at an angle.

'Oi!' James exclaimed, rubbing his head.

Edith tore at her frizzy hair in frustration as the

boy then slowly ambled down the pitch to get the winning goal St Sebastian's needed.

'That's *definitely* the last straw!' she cried. 'I've had enough!'

She looked around wildly. The team was terrified. Matt was trying to climb up a goalpost to escape. Ahmed was waving a corner flag around his head like a spear.

'I'm going to have to finish them off the old-fashioned way!' Edith muttered, scanning the pitch. 'Now, who's going to get it first, eh?' she cackled. 'Who wants to taste the Codd fury?'

Halfway across the pitch, Lenny seemed to have got over his initial terror and was standing alone by the centre circle, picking his nose.

'Aha!' Edith cried. 'The perfect victim!'

With a screech and a wail, she ruffled up her hair – loosening a cloud of dandruff – and made herself fully visible.

Lenny turned to see what all the noise was about, and froze on the spot. Advancing towards him was the most terrifying sight he had ever seen. It was – or had once been – an old woman. But she was as thin as a skeleton, white as a sheet, and had what looked like a bunch of fuzzy red snakes sticking out at all angles from her head.

He staggered backwards, reeling with shock.

'James!' he cried, finding his voice at last. 'Get over here – *now!*'

Edith carried on lurching towards him, bits of her skin flaking off as she moved her bony legs. She was plastered in crusty sewage, and a stinking green smoke was hissing out of her ears like steam.

'OI! JAMES!' Lenny bellowed. '*Do* something!'

The old hag broke into a run and opened her mouth in a hideous grin. Two rotten stumps poked out where her front teeth should be, and her eyes glowed a fiery red. A gruesome, shrill cackle rang out across the sports field.

James watched, helpless, from the other end of the pitch.

'Run, Lenny!' he yelled, as the beast flew towards his friend. 'Or hit it! Or *something*!'

Lenny turned to flee, but slipped in the mud and fell over. He scrabbled around trying to get up, and slipped again.

'Aaaaargh!' he cried. 'Go away! Get off me!'

Edith was almost upon him, her gnarled hands stretched out ready to clasp round Lenny's neck.

'Ha, ha, ha!' she croaked in her grating voice. 'There's no escape now, boy!'

James looked around frantically for a weapon. In desperation, he picked up the football and hoofed it as hard as he could in Edith's direction.

'Take *that*!' he cried. 'And get off my mate!'

At the same moment, Ambrose stopped examining his leech tin and looked up to see Edith bearing down on Lenny.

'Oh, for goodness' sake!' he muttered, jogging over to Lenny's side. 'There's never a moment's peace around here!'

Keeping himself invisible, he calmly stuck out his foot as Edith screamed past. She tripped on it, flew into the air, and careered right over Lenny's terrified, quivering body.

'AAAAAAAAAARGH!' Lenny screamed, covering his head with his hands.

'SCRRRRROARGH!' Edith screeched in fury, flying through the air over him.

'Heh!' smirked Ambrose, returning to his leech-es. 'That'll show her!'

Lenny peeked through his fingers just in time to see the flying football smash into Edith's face be-fore she landed with a thud on the ground be-hind him. As she hit the mud, she turned invisible again, and everything went silent.

Lenny got to his feet slowly. Everyone on the pitch was staring at him aghast.

'Well, thanks a bunch for coming to the rescue, you lot!' he said, sarcastically. 'It's lucky that . . . that . . . *thing* tripped up, or I'd've been ghost food!'

Matt looked sheepishly down from his perch on the crossbar.

'Sorry, mate,' he said, 'but that was gruesome!'

Ahmed was still too scared to speak, but he nodded furiously in agreement.

'Oh, and here's the heroic James Simpson!' Lenny carried on, scowling at James. 'You were a fat lot of good! Was booting the ball at it all you could think of?'

100

James shrugged. 'Well, I knew something would crop up, and it did, so why are you moaning?'

Lenny gave him a shove. 'I'll remember that next time you need *your* life saved. What *was* that thing, anyway?'

Everyone turned round to look at the spot were Edith had landed. All that remained was a dent in the mud and the football – which had bounced off her head and rolled into the back of the empty St Mary's goal.

'Dunno!' said James, stroking his chin. 'But whatever it was, it just scored us the winning goal!'

Lenny turned to his friend. 'Amazing. I nearly die at the hands of a supernatural monster, and you're still thinking about football.'

James smiled at him. 'Well, we've won, haven't we?' he said.

'Why are you so calm?' cried Lenny, his hands on his hips. 'Anyway, we only won because the St Mary's team legged it back to their minibus halfway through the second half!'

James tutted. 'A win's a win, no matter how you get it!' he said. 'Speaking of which, where's the ref? It must be full time by now!'

Ahmed coughed and pointed to a nearby tree. Almost at the top, curled in a ball, rocking back and forth, was the terrified referee.

'Erm, are you OK, ref?' called James, approaching the tree slowly. 'D'you want a hand down from there?'

The referee shook his head. 'No chance!' he whimpered. 'There's no *way* I'm coming down! Those . . . those . . . *things* might still be there!'

James sighed. 'Well, any chance you could blow the whistle for full time then?' he asked, giving the tree trunk a kick.

The referee gripped the branch he was on with one hand, and fumbled his whistle to his mouth with the other.

'Ph-ph-pheeeeeeep!'

The cup final was officially over.

103

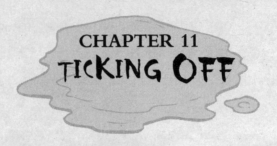

CHAPTER 11
TICKING OFF

'Blast!' Mr Tick exclaimed, smashing his computer mouse on his desk. 'That's three games in a row I've lost now!'

He closed down the solitaire window on his computer and looked at his watch with a sigh.

'Miss Keys!' he called to the school secretary. 'I'm going to go and dish out some punishment to that useless year-seven football team!'

Miss Keys appeared at the door of his office, holding his St Sebastian's scarf.

'Will you be wanting this, Mr Tick?' she smiled.

Mr Tick just frowned at her.

'Certainly not!' he grumbled. 'Our football team is an embarrassment. I don't want anyone from St Mary's recognising me as their headmaster!'

He strode out of the office, slamming the door on a flustered-looking Miss Keys.

'Useless kids!' he hissed under his breath.

Mr Tick was sick of the St Mary's headmaster, Mr Cross, gloating about his football team. The man teased him about the St Sebastian's team's poor performance every year at the annual headmasters' dinner dance at the town hall, and he could never do a thing about it.

'Detentions are too good for them!' he continued under his breath, as he stomped out on to the field.

But what he saw as he approached the football pitch surprised him. Instead of the St Mary's team dancing round celebrating with their supporters, the field was almost empty.

'What's going on here?' he roared, as he reached the touchline. 'Where is everybody?'

He looked around, but there was no sign of

the St Mary's team. Or any supporters or St Sebastian's teachers; in fact, there wasn't a single adult anywhere to be seen.

Mr Tick frowned.

'You, boy!' he shouted at Lenny, who had James in a headlock. 'Stop that at once and tell me what's going on here!'

Lenny let James go, but not before giving his neck one final squeeze.

'Nothing, sir!' he mumbled. 'I was just, erm, helping James with some stretches!'

Mr Tick scowled. 'I'm not talking about that, you fool!' he said. 'I mean, where *is* everybody? And why is the referee up that tree? And what was the final score, anyway?' he added.

Lenny scowled. 'Maybe if you'd bothered to *watch* the match, you'd know!' he grumbled.

James nudged him to shut him up. 'What Lenny means, sir,' he said, sucking up to Mr Tick, 'is that everyone's gone home. But we won, sir, eleven–ten!'

Mr Tick raised his eyebrows in surprise. 'You won?' he said. '*Really?*'

James and Lenny nodded.

'Yes, sir! Our team really came out fighting in the second half!' Lenny smirked.

James nudged Lenny again. 'What Lenny means, sir, is that we played a lot better after half-time!' he said.

Mr Tick nodded and puffed out his chest.

'Well, I have to say I'm very impressed with you all. Very impressed indeed!' he said, surveying the St Sebastian's team. 'And, yes, that includes you, Alexander!' he said, looking over at the goal.

'Alexander?' he called out. 'Are you OK?'

The ghostly Alexander was propped up against a goalpost, looking paler than ever. In fact, he was almost transparent. Mr Tick approached slowly.

'I said, are you OK, Alexander?'

He reached what he thought was his son, and

put out a hand to pat him on the head. The boy looked up at him with hollow, black eyes. What looked like slime was dripping off his hair and arms and, as Mr Tick went to pat him, a maggot slithered round the side of his head and dropped on to his shoulder.

'Eugh!' Mr Tick cried, pulling his hand away. 'We need a chat about your personal hygiene, Alexander!' he said, sternly.

'He's just, erm, tired after the match, sir!' James called out.

Mr Tick shrugged and started walking back to his office. For the first time in years, he could look forward to the annual headmasters' dinner dance. He would wear his St Sebastian's scarf just to annoy Mr Cross, he thought, spitefully.

'Heh, heh!' Mr Tick laughed to himself. 'I can just imagine Mr Cross's face right now!' he sniggered. 'He must be furious!'

Behind him, in the car park, Mr Cross had that face pressed up against the window of the St Mary's minibus. The rest of the team were piled behind him, straining to see what was going on outside. They all looked absolutely terrified.

'Drive! Drive!' Mr Cross was bellowing at the driver. 'It's following us!'

Next to the bus, a man with no head was riding a huge, black horse. He was holding his severed head at arm's length, and it was blowing big raspberries at the faces behind the glass.

109

'Losers!' it called. 'You were all rubbish!'

The St Mary's bus lurched forwards, its tyres squealing. The Headless Horseman followed it, blowing more raspberries.

'Losers! Weaklings!' he cried, over the muffled screams coming from the minibus.

Mr Tick carried on walking the other way, lost in his own little world.

'Now!' he said, to no one in particular. 'Time to celebrate with a nice game of solitaire . . .'

He strode into his office past his secretary.

'Don't let anyone disturb me, Miss Keys!' he said, sternly. 'I have some very important work to attend to!'

Ambrose laughed as the Headless Horseman charged after the St Mary's coach.

'Oh, come on!' he chuckled. 'Leave them alone!'

The Headless Horseman reared on his horse and strolled back to Ambrose.

'Bah!' the horseman grumbled. 'Spoil sport!'

'Nonsense!' cried Ambrose, slapping him on the back. 'But we'd better get back to the plague pit: Edith's going to take a *lot* of calming down!'

'You said it!' the horseman sighed. 'Shall we pick up William on the way?'

Ambrose shook his head. 'Nah!' he replied,

looking over to the pitch where James was slapping the goalie on the back. 'Let him have
a few more minutes of fun!'

The two older ghosts floated into the boys' toilet block and started squeezing themselves down
one of the filthy toilet bowls.

In the main sewer at the other end, Ambrose
spat out some gruesome slime and popped a
leech in his mouth to take the taste away.

The Headless Horseman dropped down next,
bending to pick up his head that he'd dropped
down the pipe ahead of him.

'Right,' shuddered Ambrose. 'Let's find Edith
and see what the damage is!'

CHAPTER 12
GOODBYE, GHOULIE

James, Lenny and the ghostly Alexander watched Mr Tick stride off towards the school.

'Well, at least we aren't facing a month of de-tentions!' said James.

'Yeah, that's definitely the biggest relief of the afternoon!' Lenny replied, sarcastically. 'Oh – except for *escaping with my life*, that is!'

James groaned. 'Moan, moan, moan!' he said, rolling his eyes. 'I'm going to send your name to the *Guinness Book of Records*. World's biggest moaner: Lenny Maxwell. Undisputed moaning champion for the last eleven years!'

Lenny scowled. 'Oh, yeah? Well, I'll send your name in then. World's biggest sucker-upper: James Simpson. "Yes, Mr Tick, sir, we played great, Mr Tick, sir! Please like me, Mr Tick, sir!"' he mimicked, skipping in a circle around James and flapping his hands about.

'Right, that's it!' James laughed, putting his fists up like a boxer. Then he stopped and looked over at the goal.

'Whoah!' he said, as Lenny turned round to see what he was staring at. 'Are you OK there?'

Before their very eyes, something strange was happening to their ghostly goalie. He was groaning quietly, and his whole body was turning transparent. They could even see the goalpost through his thin body!

Lenny approached him slowly. 'What's happening?' he asked the ghost. 'Do you need help?'

William shook his head and looked at his two new friends. He was finding it increasingly hard to maintain his Alexander disguise, and he knew he'd vanish from sight completely any minute.

'Wow!' James said to Lenny. 'You can see right through him!'

William smiled weakly and faded a little more. He was as happy as he could remember being since he'd died. He'd had a great day playing football and, above all, being part of the real, live St Sebastian's football team!

James had to squint to make him out because he was so faint.

'Bye, mate!' he shouted at the vanishing ghost. 'And thanks for helping us win!'

Lenny just stood there, open-mouthed, watching the boy vanish before him.

William beamed. James had called him 'mate'! He'd been one of the gang – even if it had only been for a day! With a final grin, he faded into invisibility and turned towards the main building.

The boys stared at the spot where their goalie had been standing. James wafted his hand through the air. The ghoul was gone.

'He really has vanished!' he cried.

'You know what the scary thing is?' said Lenny, calmly. 'That really isn't the strangest thing I've seen today!'

James nodded. 'I'll kind of miss him, you know,' he said. 'He certainly made the game more fun!'

Lenny turned to face him and put his hands on his hips.

'More fun?' he said, angrily. '*You* obviously didn't have some bloodthirsty ghoul trying to kill you during the match. I wouldn't call that fun!'

James just laughed. 'There you go again – moan, moan moan!'

'You saw that shrieking ghost. You're telling me you wouldn't have been scared?' Lenny argued.

'Yes, of course I saw her. And she *was* terrifying!' smirked James. 'But no more scary than seeing your grandma in her nightie!'

Lenny gasped and made a swipe at James. 'Oi! Leave my grandma out of this!' he scowled, pretending to be mortally offended.

James neatly ducked out of the way. 'All I'm saying,' he continued, giggling, 'is, are you sure it wasn't actually her? Maybe you forgot your dinner money and your grandma wanted to give it to you or something . . . AAAAAARGH!'

Lenny landed a punch on the top of James's arm.

'That should shut you up!' Lenny sniggered.

James rubbed his arm. 'No need to get violent,' he grumbled. 'After all, it was my great shot that saved you from the beast!'

Lenny raised his eyebrows. 'Pure luck she tripped up, more like!' he replied.

'Anyway,' James said, 'we all made it through the match, and that's what counts. And what's more, we won! Now – how about a game of keepie-uppie before we go home?'

Lenny rolled his eyes. 'Get lost!' he said. 'I've definitely had enough football for one day! And anyway, don't you think it might be time to liberate Alexander from that cupboard you stuffed him in?'

'Stick!' James cried, slapping his forehead. 'I completely forgot about him! Let's go!'

'No rush though,' Lenny added, smirking. 'I

mean, it *has* been nice to have a joke-free after-noon . . .'

James laughed. 'Yeah, you're right – and I haven't heard a single scientific theory since the match began!' he joked.

As they reached the door to the changing room, they could hear Alexander banging about inside the cupboard, desperate to escape. James began to unwedge the chair that was holding it shut.

'Well, I'd like to hear science explain what just happened on that football pitch!' Lenny said, kicking his boots off.

'Oh, I'm sure Alexander will have a theory!' James laughed. 'Once we've got him out of here, you can tell him all about it!'

As he spoke, a bundle of smelly clothes, football boots and a very red-faced headmaster's son tumbled out of the cupboard and into a heap on the floor.

'James Simpson!' he hissed furiously. 'You'd better have an absolutely amazing explanation

for locking me up, or there'll be BIG trouble!'

James grinned. 'Actually, Stick, we have got a rather good excuse.'

He turned to Lenny on the bench behind him. 'Well?' he laughed, as Alexander continued to stare up at him from the floor. 'Do you want to tell him, or shall I?'

Lenny puffed his cheeks out and whistled.

'I don't know where to begin,' he said. 'But I'll say one thing, Alexander – I'll never moan about you being in goal again!'

CHAPTER 13
WELL PLAGUED

William jogged happily back towards the toilet block, but the nearer he got to it, the gloomier he felt. Sure, he'd had a brilliant day, but he knew he was going to have to pay for it at the hands of Edith Codd.

'She'll be extra annoyed now that St Sebastian's have won!' he groaned, as he squeezed himself into a dirty toilet bowl. 'I hate to think what gruesome punishment she's thought up for me . . . mumph!'

William swallowed a mouthful of grot as he wriggled through the U-bend. He dropped down into the main sewer and brushed himself down.

'Blurgh! Ugh!' he spat, as he wiped his eyes.

He sat down on a rusty pipe, leant his head against the cold sewer wall, and shut his eyes tight. He calculated it would take Edith roughly thirty seconds to find him.

'Ha, ha, ha!'

He heard a familiar sound echo down the tunnel in front of him, making the hairs on his neck stand on end.

'Here she comes!' William said to himself.

'Ha, ha, haaa!' Edith's dry, drain-like laugh bounced off the pipes and brickwork. William kept his eyes clamped shut.

'This is it!' he muttered. 'Aaaargh!'

Something cold and scratchy had touched his foot. William froze.

'Ha, ha, haaaaa!'

He opened one eye slowly and looked down. Phew. It was just a rat nibbling at his shoe. Several others were scuttling along the sewer away from Edith's horrible cackling.

William kept his eyes open and looked about. A wave of rats fled from the direction of the amphitheatre, almost bowling William over. Even *they* couldn't bear the sound of her.

'Whoah!' he cried, just managing to keep his balance. 'Easy there!'

'Ha, ha, haaaaaaaaaaa!'

William gulped, and began to follow the noise.

'Might as well get this over with!' he said to himself. 'I can't take this suspense!'

He ambled slowly along, following the gruesome echo. After a few minutes, it led him to the amphitheatre. As he approached, Edith's voice got louder and he could hear her holding court.

'She's probably ranting about me,' William muttered. 'She's probably telling the others what terrible punishment she's got in mind for me . . .'

He trudged round the corner and into the amphitheatre, his hands deep in his pockets and his head hung low. All traces of the day's excitement had disappeared from his face.

'WILLIAM SCROGGINS!' Edith croaked, as he slouched into the cavern. '*Just* the person I want to see!'

William groaned and looked up. Edith was standing on her upturned ranting barrel surrounded by a crowd of ghosts. Her eyes glowed bright, and her vile red hair stood on end.

'Coming, Edith!' he sighed.

What will the punishment be? he thought to himself. *Being locked in the rat hole? A week under the sewage outlet? A day in the maggot pit?*

Edith drew herself up to her full height and pointed a rotten, flaky finger at William.

'This boy here . . .' she began, gesturing wildly towards William, 'saw the whole thing!'

The young ghost stared at his shoes. As if being punished wasn't enough, he was going to have to sit through a rant as well!

'Yes, indeed! He saw me score the amazing *winning goal*!' Edith screeched. 'Didn't you, lad?' She reached down and ruffled his hair, giving him a friendly wink.

'Wh-wh-what?' William stuttered, looking up at her, confused.

'My *goal*!' she screamed. 'My diving header – to win the match! You saw it, didn't you? Well – tell everyone how good it was!'

William's jaw dropped. Edith, rather than being furious, seemed deliriously happy! He closed his mouth and slowly turned to the assembled ghosts.

'Er, yeah – it was great, Edith!' he smirked with relief. 'Brilliant goal!'

Edith beamed a brown-toothed grin.

'I told you all!' she howled. 'I'm a great sportswoman! Almost professional standard! The crowd *loved* me!'

At the back of the room, Ambrose rolled his eyes. William snuck through the throng of ghosts and appeared at his side.

'I come from a family of sportspeople,' Edith continued. 'My father was the Great Smithing-

ton badger-wrestling champion of thirteen-twenty-nine. And now I'm a footballing heroine!'

Ambrose nudged William. 'Didn't the ball just bounce off her head as she fell over?' he chuckled.

'It was one of the worst goals I've ever seen!'

William nodded.

'Yeah, but I'm not complaining!' he whispered back. 'Her good mood seems to have got me right off the hook!'

The Headless Horseman's head rolled quietly up to William and Ambrose, stopping at their feet.

'I can't take much more of this rubbish!' it complained. 'Can we get out of here, please?'

Ambrose laughed. 'How about a game of footy?' he suggested. 'And I mean *real* footy, not that namby-pamby version they play up there!'

William grabbed the horseman's head under his arm and set off with Ambrose.

'Sure thing!' he smiled. 'On one condition!'

'What's that?' Ambrose asked, looking puzzled.

William laughed. 'That that battleaxe doesn't join us!'

As they disappeared up a sewage pipe, they could hear Edith working herself up into a frenzy.

'St Sebastian's!' she wailed. 'You'd be nothing

without me! Nothing, you hear!'

A hundred metres above her head, Mr Tick glanced up from his computer at the water pipe that ran up one corner of his office.

'That's odd!' he said to himself. 'They're making a rather funny noise!'

129

He pressed his ear against it and listened hard. The noise was almost like a faint, gurgling voice.

'I won you the match, St Sebastian's!' it said, to Mr Tick's surprise. 'I won the cup final for you!'

Mr Tick shook his head to try and clear it.

'I'm hearing things!' he said to himself. 'Must be the stress! Too much hard work.'

He rubbed his eyes and stretched his mouse finger.

'What I need is a break!' he muttered, looking warily at the water pipe across the room. 'This calls for a nice game of solitaire . . .'

SURNAME: Horseman

FIRST NAME: Headless

AGE: 394

HEIGHT: 1.5 metres without head; 1.8 metres with head

EYES: Red and glowing

HAIR: Used as a makeshift handle to carry head around

LIKES: A game of football; horse riding; old civil war stories

DISLIKES: The inconvenience of carrying his head about; the funny looks he gets from other ghosts

SPECIAL SKILL: Can roll his head round corners to see things other ghosts can't see!

INTERESTING FACT: The Headless Horseman didn't die of the plague like the other ghosts; he was beheaded in the civil war in 1643, and has been roaming around with his head tucked under his arm ever since

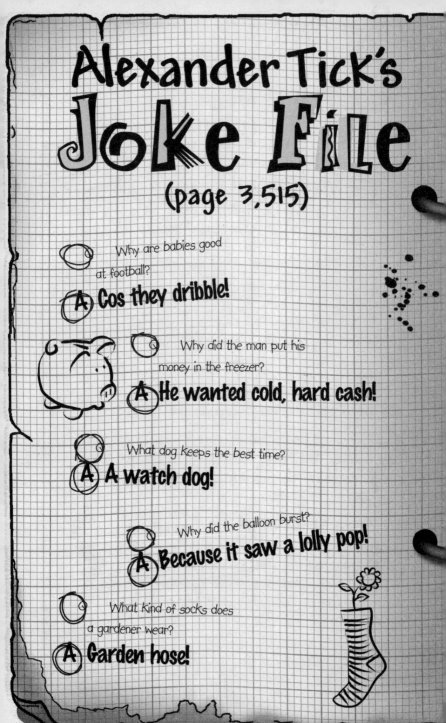

Medieval Football:

The Facts!

What was footy like when William was alive?

In 1314, the mayor of London banned football completely cos it caused so much damage.

Modern football rules weren't invented until the 1800s. In the 1300s, there were hardly any rules and no referees.

There were no limits on team size in medieval times. Your whole village could play on one team!

There were no special football pitches. Games took place in fields, through towns, and often caused lots of damage on the way.

Kicking, punching and other ways to get your opponent off the ball were all allowed!

There was no time limit for games – they could go on for hours!

Different towns, schools and villages all had different rules for football, so they had to agree on the rules before every game.

In some rough matches, the only rule was that the players weren't allowed to murder each other!

Ten Reasons Why a Ghost Makes a Great Goalie

By William Scroggins, St Sebastian's goalkeeping hero

1. Light, bony body good at floating through the air

2. Ability to disappear scares opposition – and everyone else!

3. Much tougher than those wimpy modern goalies

4. Ghosts don't need half-time oranges

5. Namby-pamby modern refs ignore ghosts' fouls

6. Everyone was a rush goalie in the old days

7. A bit of slime can come in handy on the football pitch

8. Can't get injured as already dead

9. Can call up extra spirits if team is losing

10. Ghosts look excellent in team photos

Downsides: Bit scary in the team bath . . .

Can't wait for the next book in the series?

Here's a sneak preview of

A FÊTE WORSE THAN DEATH

CHAPTER 1
NEW BALLS, PLEASE

'Lenny, Lenny! To me!'

Lenny Maxwell leapt into the air and punched the volleyball across the court towards his friend and teammate James Simpson. With only one point between the teams, this would be the shot that finally drew year-seven's Thunderbolts level with their year-eight rival team, The Stingrays.

James flicked his floppy brown fringe out of his eyes and launched himself off the ground in a jump timed perfectly to achieve the maximum height as the ball sailed towards him. Just a metre away, over the net, Jason Yates also jumped,

arms raised to try and block James's return shot.

The two athletes' eyes met. Both were determined to win this rally and claim victory for their team. And both knew whatever happened next would change the outcome of the match, and the St Sebastian's boys' volleyball league.

Alexander Tick dashed into position beside James, fists clenched to return any smash that Jason might be about to make. He gritted his teeth and watched as, almost in slow motion, the volleyball spun through the air and hung, for the briefest of moments, directly over James's head.

Jason could only stare as James's right hand whipped up from his side and lashed out for the ball. Skin made contact with leather as the Thunderbolts' top scorer smashed his palm into the ball . . . and the ball exploded, wrapping James's whole fist with what was left of the warm, sweat-soaked piece of sports equipment.

'Eurgh! Get it off!' wailed James, crashing back to the floor and shaking his hand to try and free it. Lenny ran over and peeled the dead ball from his friend's fingers.

'Looks like the sticking plaster covering the puncture came unstuck,' said Alexander, trotting across the sports hall to the equipment cupboard to find the first-aid kit. 'I'll get another one.'

Carefully opening the battered old tin so as not to disturb its flaking paint, he rooted through its contents.

'There aren't any left!' he called over, to the disappointment of the volleyball players. 'Just an old, brown bandage and a bottle of painkillers filled with gummy bears.'

'Gummy bears?' questioned Lenny. 'What use are they if you've got an injury?'

'Actually, the effects of placebo medicines are well documented,' replied Alexander, as he rejoined his teammates. 'The psychosomatic results they achieve can often be compared favourably to those of genuine pharmaceutical products.'

Lenny blinked. 'Why don't you ever talk properly?' he asked.

James smiled. 'What Stick means is that if you just *think* you're taking a painkiller, it sometimes has the same effect as actually taking one.'

Lenny rubbed at his forehead. 'In that case, hand me the gummy bears; I'm getting a headache just listening to him.'

The peep of a whistle interrupted James's laugh

as Ms Legg, the PE teacher, strode across the sports hall towards the two teams. 'Why have you boys stopped playing?' she demanded.

Alexander held up the remains of the volleyball. 'Problem with the equipment, miss,' he said. 'Have we got another one?'

Ms Legg shook her head. 'The only things left in the equipment cupboard are an oval hula hoop and a couple of bamboo garden canes we've been using for javelins.'

'And don't forget the vaulting horse that's so past its prime it's been put out to grass!' quipped Alexander, glancing from blank face to blank face as he searched for someone who'd share what he thought passed for a joke.

Ms Legg sighed. 'I swear, if you weren't the headmaster's son we'd have buried you in the long-jump pit months ago,' she mumbled under her breath. 'Right!' she continued, pausing to let loose another sharp blast on her whistle to get everyone's attention. 'Consider this game cancelled; you can fill the remaining lesson time by doing laps of the sports hall.'

Ignoring the groans of 'Oh, Miss!', Ms Legg marched purposefully out of the sports hall. The neglect of the PE department had gone on for long enough.

When the telephone rang, Miss Keys, the school secretary, jumped and pricked her finger for the fifteenth time that morning.

She sighed and put down her needle and thread. Some of these lab coats were simply beyond repair; why couldn't Mr Tick just accept the fact? As much as she admired him, sometimes the headmaster could be a real penny-pincher.

After the phone conversation, Miss Keys buzzed through to the headmaster on the intercom – although intercom was a rather flattering description for the recently replaced system. What sat on Miss Keys's desk was one half of a second-hand baby monitor with the words 'Daddy's Little Princess' scribbled out with marker pen.

'Yes, Miss Keys?' droned the headmaster's voice through the tiny speaker, making the pink bunny on the front of the monitor light up. 'I'm at an important stage in my solitaire game right now. Can this wait?'

'I'm afraid not, Mr Tick,' replied the secretary. 'Ms Legg has telephoned to ask for some new sports equipment.'

'What?!' roared the pink bunny. 'Does she think I'm made of money?'

'That's not all, sir,' continued Miss Keys. 'I've also had calls this morning from Mr Drew saying the piano's got so many keys missing that the school orchestra can't follow the tune he's playing; Mr Parker wanting new batteries for the maths department's only calculator; and Mr Hall demanding to know why the new history textbooks you bought suddenly stop after the Battle of Hastings.'

Mr Tick appeared in the doorway that linked his office to the secretary's.

'This is ridiculous!' he snapped. 'Whatever happened to the days when all you needed to be a teacher was a piece of chalk and a can-do attitude?'

'They ended when these lab coats were in fashion, sir,' smiled Miss Keys, as she stitched what had been part of a tablecloth on to one of the long, pointy collars.

It was obvious from Mr Tick's expression that he failed to see the joke.

'If we need extra money, why don't we hold some sort of school fête?' suggested Miss Keys. 'We could sell home-made plum jam and have a three-legged race!'

Mr Tick nodded slowly. 'The idea has merit,' he agreed, 'despite your talk of tasteless jam and stupid races. But it all just seems a lot of hard work which, frankly, I'm too important to be bothered with!'

Then a sly smile lit up the headmaster's face. 'However, the pupils aren't important at all. They shall organise the fête!'